Elijah Wood

Hollywood's Hottest Rising Star

LISA DEGNEN

WARNER BOOKS

A Time Warner Company

If you purchase this book without a cover you should be aware that this book may have been stolen property and reported as "unsold and destroyed" to the publisher. In such case neither the author nor the publisher has received any payment for this "stripped book."

Copyright © 1999 Michael Friedman Publishing Group, Inc.
All rights reserved.

Warner Books, Inc.
1271 Avenue of the Americas
New York, NY 10020
Visit our Web site at www.warnerbooks.com

A Time Warner Company

Printed in the United States of America

First Printing: May 1999

10 9 8 7 6 5 4 3 2 1

ISBN: 0-446-67581-4
LC: 99-60267

Editor: Emily Zelner
Art Director: Jeff Batzli
Designer: Millie Sensat
Photography Editor: Valerie E. Kennedy
Production Manager: Camille Lee

CONTENTS

Introduction
page 8

Chapter One
How It All Began
page 10

Chapter Two
Elijah Up Close and Personal
page 20

Chapter Three
The Road to Superstardom
page 34

Chapter Four
The Road Ahead
page 86

Filmography
page 92

Bibliography
page 93

Index
page 95

INTRODUCTION

Elijah Wood is one of the hottest young talents in the world, but he's still managed to remain a normal, down-to-earth guy who loves his family and friends, as well as his two dogs, Rascal and Levi.

This book doesn't tell you everything there is to know about Elijah—he'd have to tell you that himself—but you'll find all you have to know to call yourself a true fan on the pages ahead.

There's a lot to know about this complicated, interesting, and adorable star—so start reading!

ABOVE: ELIJAH HAPPILY PROMOTED *NORTH* IN 1994. HE WAS WIDELY PRAISED AS THE BEST PART OF THE MOVIE. OPPOSITE: ALREADY AN OLD PRO AT DEALING WITH THE PRESS, ELIJAH WAS ALL SMILES WHILE HE WAS PROMOTING *THE FACULTY* IN 1998.

The Complete Elijah Wood Fact File

NAME: Elijah Jordan Wood

HAIR: Brown

EYES: Blue

HEIGHT: 5' 6"

BIRTHDATE: January 28, 1981

BIRTHPLACE: Cedar Rapids, Iowa

PARENTS: Warren and Debbie

OLDER BROTHER: Zach

YOUNGER SISTER: Hannah

FAVORITE BOOK: *The Hobbit*

FAVORITE COLOR: Blue

FAVORITE HOBBIES: Singing, fencing, Rollerblading, swimming, reading, cooking, and collecting *Star Wars* memorabilia. "I love to read. I know that my acting has been enriched by reading. It allows you to understand human nature and what people are all about."

NICKNAME: "Monkey" or "The Funny"

PETS: Bearded collies Rascal and Levi

BAD HABIT: Bites his fingernails

SCHOOL: Elijah is tutored at home or on the set of most of the movies he works on.

INSTRUMENTS: "I don't play any instruments now. But, in the past, I have gone to piano classes. I did that for almost a year. And when I worked on *North* I received a guitar and I would love to learn how to play."

FAVORITE SUBJECTS: English and History

AWARDS: ShoWest Award—Young Star of the Year (1994)

Saturn Award—Best Juvenile Performance (1994)

Young Star Award nominee (1995)

Where to Write to Him:

Elijah Wood, c/o William Morris Agency

151 El Camino Drive

Beverly Hills, CA 90212

CHAPTER ONE: HOW IT ALL BEGAN

From Cedar Rapids to Hollywood

A lot of kids who live in Cedar Rapids, Iowa, dream of growing up to be a movie star, but for most it stays a dream. Elijah Wood made his fondest dreams come true—and all before the age of twenty.

For the first few years of his life, he was just like any other kid in Cedar Rapids. Once he started school, however, his enormous talents really began to show. In 1987, he joined the chorus in his elementary school's production of *The Sound of Music*. The next year, Elijah was cast in the title role of a production of *The Wizard of Oz*.

He loved singing and dancing and his talent for acting was already evident. So when Elijah's mom, Debbie, saw a TV commercial one day, she thought to herself, "My baby could do that." In 1988, she decided to enroll her young son in a Cedar Rapids modeling school called Avant Studios. It was only a few months until seven-year-old Elijah was going on auditions and studio calls.

One of those trips took Elijah and his mom to Los Angeles for the International Modeling and Talent Association's convention. Since it was the first time they had ever stepped foot in California, it was a big trip for both of them—and one that would change their lives forever. "When my mom brought me to Hollywood for the convention, I didn't think of acting because I was just a model," Elijah remembers. "But when Gary Scalzo [who later became Elijah's talent manager] asked me if I wanted to be an actor, I said, 'Yeah sure. I'll be an actor.' Gary was one of the judges in the talent auditions, and my mom said it was OK with her. He said, 'I believe in you,' and asked my mom if we could move out here."

Gary Scalzo recalls there were about 500 kids who had turned up for the convention, but he could see Elijah's enormous talent from the start. In fact, he thought the kid might even have too much energy! Recognizing in Elijah that natural charisma often called "star quality," Gary knew he had to sign him up right away.

"It was only a few days before his eighth birthday when I saw him perform his monologue," Gary says. "It was evident that Elijah was talented

IN 1994, AT AGE THIRTEEN, ELIJAH ALREADY HAD THE LOOK THAT SETS GIRLS' HEARTS ON FIRE.

Fun Facts
How much do you know about Elijah Wood? Test your knowledge.

1. Where was the movie *North* filmed?

* Even though it's set in Alaska, the movie was actually filmed in Culver City, California.

2. What is Elijah's favorite foreign city?

* London

3. What's Elijah's favorite store to shop in?

* Banana Republic (He likes casual clothes in soft, muted shades.)

4. What was Elijah's favorite musical?

* *Les Miserables*

5. What happened to Elijah on the set of *The War*?

* They chopped off all of Elijah's beautiful, long brown hair and gave him a crew-cut!

6. Why did Elijah really love doing commercials for Wavy Lays potato chips?

* He got to meet and hang out with football great Troy Aikman. He also worked with Vice President Dan Quayle and actor Jack Palance in the ads.

7. What does Elijah do every evening?

* "You can laugh if you want, but every night my family and I watch *Extra!* and *Entertainment Tonight*," Elijah says. "I just love Mary Hart! She makes me laugh."

8. How much money does Elijah make per picture?

* He earns at least $1.5 million.

9. What's the worst lie Elijah has ever told?

* "Oh jeez!" Elijah says, "The worst kind of lying I've ever done is keeping things from people."

10. Did Elijah ever get upset about losing a part?

* He actually has cried only twice over losing a part. Once it was over a TV pilot and once it was over losing a part in the movie version of *The Secret Garden*. "There are times when I get too worked up," he says. "Then I feel bad."

11. What was the first musical group that Elijah collected?

* He has all of The Beatles CDs. "I just love their music," he says.

12. What stuffed animals does Elijah collect?

* He has a collection of stuffed monkeys because his family's nickname for him is "Monkey."

13. What kind of business did Elijah's family run in Cedar Rapids?

* They owned a deli that they sold so the whole family could move to Burbank for Elijah's career.

14. His parents call him Monkey, but what's his pals' nickname for him?

* "Lij"

15. Who was Elijah's childhood idol?
* George Lucas, who created *Star Wars*.

16. What happened after *Flipper* had wrapped up production?
* The producers had to call the entire cast back for a reshoot because the studio had arranged an $18 million product placement deal. So instead of a big scene in a Chinese restaurant, the scene was reshot at a Pizza Hut.

17. What kind of movies are Elijah's favorite?
*He really loves horror movies.

18. What kind of books does Elijah like to read?
* His favorites are science fiction, mystery, and adventure novels. But he also admits that he loved *The Hunchback of Notre Dame*. "I was so enthralled," he says. "I couldn't put it down. My other favorite is *Dracula*."

19. What does Elijah like to tell people when they tell him he's a star?
*He usually says: "I'm not a star. A star is nothing but a ball of gas."

20. Who are Elijah's favorite actor and actress?
*Tim Roth and Emma Thompson

ELIJAH'S PARENTS HAVE ALWAYS TAKEN GREAT PRIDE IN THE FACT THAT EVEN THOUGH HE IS FAMOUS, ELIJAH IS JUST AS NORMAL AND DOWN-TO-EARTH AS ANY OTHER KID.

and enjoyed what he was doing, which is important. After the competition, I talked to his mother and asked if Elijah would like to come to my office with her the next day and talk about the possibilities of an acting career. Elijah and I read some scenes together, and he was wonderful. He read brilliantly. He's also very directable."

Not long after that, the whole family moved to Los Angeles where Elijah started his fantastic career. Most actors start very slowly, moving from audition to audition and facing endless rejection and disappointment. That certainly wasn't Elijah's experience, though. Just six months after arriving in L.A., he landed his first job, in Paula Abdul's "Forever Your Girl" video.

Forever Your Girl

Today, millions of girls everywhere would love to utter those words to Elijah Wood, but it was singer and actress Paula Abdul who sang them loud and clear when he costarred in her "Forever Your Girl" video.

IN 1990, ELIJAH CAUGHT THE ATTENTION OF MOVIEGOERS WHEN HE PLAYED OPPOSITE ARMIN MUELLER STAHL IN BARRY LEVINSON'S *AVALON*.

ABOVE: ELIJAH WAS JUST NINE YEARS OLD WHEN HE MADE *AVALON*, AND HE WAS ALREADY BEING PRAISED FOR HIS ACTING TALENTS. PAGES 16–17: ELIJAH AND AIDAN QUINN, ELIJAH'S ON-SCREEN DAD IN *AVALON*, HAVE A FATHER-SON TALK.

It was a great time for both talents, who were just beginning their respective careers. Paula Julie Abdul first became famous—sort of—as one of L.A.'s popular Laker Girl cheerleaders. She was also known as a choreographer for some of the biggest acts in show business, including Michael and Janet Jackson, INXS, and for TV, *The Tracy Ullman Show*.

It's almost amazing she ever found the time to make her own records, but of course when she did, they became instant hits. *Forever Your Girl*, Abdul's first album, spawned hit songs in "Cold Hearted," "Opposites Attract," "Straight Up," and "The Way That You Love Me." But the song that really made the biggest impact was "Forever Your Girl."

In the video for "Forever Your Girl," one of his first acting jobs, Elijah took his own stab at stardom, at just eight years old playing a very junior executive. It was a pivotal moment, and his agent and talent scouts suddenly realized they had a star on their hands.

Movies like *Back to the Future Part II* and *Internal Affairs* soon followed. The film that really made people stand up and take notice of the young actor, though, was 1990's *Avalon* with Aidan Quinn. "Elijah's personality is just right for the screen," says Gary. "When he walks in, the whole room lights up."

IN 1990, ELIJAH COSTARRED WITH ACTRESS DELTA BURKE IN NBC'S *DAY-O*, WHICH WAS ONE OF HIS FIRST TELEVISION PROJECTS.

IN *DAY-O*, ELIJAH PLAYED DELTA BURKE'S IMAGINARY CHILDHOOD PLAYMATE, WHO RETURNS TO HER SIDE WHEN SHE STARTS TO WORRY THAT SHE'S LET LIFE PASS HER BY.

CHAPTER TWO
ELIJAH UP CLOSE & PERSONAL

Family Ties

Even though Elijah doesn't come from a traditional acting family, both of his siblings have tried their hand at acting. Almost immediately, Hannah decided that she didn't like show business at all and told her mom she wanted to quit. Zach, however, started acting about the same time that Elijah did, and he's done some commercials and small acting projects.

"I have a great relationship with my brother and a great relationship with my sister," Elijah says. "I like to hang out with the both of them." Elijah and Zach love to watch sports together. They especially love hockey and football and usually root for all the Los Angeles sports teams.

The entire Wood family is especially close, and the young actor credits his parents for helping him to keep his head on straight. For example, he has made millions of dollars in his career, but still gets a small allowance every week. And that's just fine with this young star. "It's really no big deal," he smiles.

AT THE *NORTH* PREMIERE IN 1994, ELIJAH INCLUDED SIS HANNAH AND HER PAL IN ALL THE CELEBRATIONS.

"Elijah's mother is the best," says agent Brian Swardstrom. "A lot of times stage mothers live through their children. If tomorrow Elijah said he didn't want to do this anymore, she would say, 'Fine, it's over, I'm glad you had the experience.'"

Elijah feels he is well-grounded and gives his close family all the credit. "My mom and my family have supported me," he

ELIJAH CREDITS HIS MOM, DEBBIE, FOR BEING THE DRIVING FORCE IN HIS LIFE AND ALSO THE ONE WHO NEVER LET FAME GO TO HIS HEAD. SHE WAS HIS DATE AT THE *PARADISE* PREMIERE IN 1991.

says. "My mom taught me to stay on the ground and not get a big head. I've been taught that way early. I want to work and enjoy working because I have wonderful parents."

Elijah has seen the downside of life in show business, especially for those who don't have a good support system at home. He worked with Macaulay Culkin in the 1993 film *The Good Son* and understands why Macaulay gave up his acting career for a while when his family started to fall apart.

"He was out of work because he didn't want to work," Elijah says of the *Home Alone* star. "He didn't work because of his parents mainly. It's a sad story. He was depressed and not living a good life."

Macaulay's parents ended up in a nasty custody fight over their famous kid, and Mac once even called the cops on his dad after he slapped him during a fight. "I don't have the type of parents he had. They went about it the wrong way," Elijah says.

To make sure that he does not become spoiled, Elijah's mom never lets him ride around in limos and he's never allowed to accept gifts over twenty dollars.

HANNAH WENT WITH ELIJAH TO SEE *THE FRIGHTENERS*. AS THEY'VE GOTTEN OLDER, ELIJAH AND HANNAH HAVE GROWN TO REALLY APPRECIATE THEIR CLOSE FRIENDSHIP.

Elijah and Hannah

Elijah and Hannah are about as close and friendly as any two siblings can be. But Hannah freely admits it hasn't always been easy being the little sister of a superstar. As the youngest of the three Wood children, Hannah has always had to tag along to every one of Elijah's film locations. In fact, it's been a part of her lifestyle for as long as she can remember. "We've been all over the country," Hannah says.

Hannah says that there have been times when all the family togetherness really got to her—especially when it meant being with her brother "twenty-four-seven."

"There was that couple of years when we hated each other," she says. "I think it was because he was getting all of the attention. Now we get along really well....We go see movies and go CD shopping."

She says that there really was a time when she would have liked to be a famous member of the family and follow in her big brother's footsteps, but she has decided that it's not for her. "I get too bashful, too giggly," she says. "I guess acting's not my thing."

ELIJAH AND HANNAH LOOKED STYLISH AT THE HOLLYWOOD PREMIERE OF *TITANIC*.

Elijah Speaks

Through the years, Elijah has talked about his life in the movies and how he has literally grown up in front of the public. We've taken the best of his interviews and compiled them into questions and answers so you can hear from your favorite star in his own words.

Q: You seem to have a lot of energy. Have you always been that way?
ELIJAH: I'm kind of a monkey. I like to jump around. I can't sit down. I just have to keep moving. I like moving and running around and having fun.

ELIJAH'S CURLY BROWN HAIR AND STRIKING BLUE EYES HAVE MELTED MORE THAN JUST A FEW GIRLS' HEARTS.

Q: Who is the person who has influenced you the most?
ELIJAH: My mom. She's great and has always kept me grounded.

Q: What do you think about being famous? Is that why you wanted to become an actor?
ELIJAH: I never wanted to act to become famous. I just enjoy acting. I wouldn't want to deal with the kind of fame where everyone recognized you everywhere you went. I don't want to be incredibly famous because it's so pointless. You don't need to be that famous. I have fun being with my family and working on films.

Q: What's the downside to fame?
ELIJAH: When we lived in Petaluma, California, everyone knew where I lived. Moms would come to my house and ask me to perform at their daughters' birthday parties. I was like, "I am not on display." I act because I enjoy it. I don't do it to be famous.

Q: Is it hard to have a normal life sometimes—to have normal friends?

ELIJAH HAS BUILT A REPUTATION AS ONE OF THE NICEST, MOST RELIABLE YOUNG STARS IN HOLLYWOOD.

ELIJAH: I don't have many friends. I've got a great family. I don't need friends right now. Most of my friends are adults, and I'm happy with that. There's a problem with having kid friends sometimes. Let's say you have a friend who wasn't in the business. I've had many. They all go downhill the first week. The kids only like you [because you're] an actor. You know how you can find that out? That's all they talk about! I have this friend who keeps calling my house and the reason he's doing it is because I'm an actor. He

ELIJAH'S FAMILY STILL CALLS HIM OCCASIONALLY BY HIS CHILDHOOD NICKNAMES "MONKEY" AND "THE FUNNY."

took a magazine and said, "Look there's a story about you, isn't that cool?" I'm like, "No! Let's go out and get some CDs. Let's not talk about this."

Q: Isn't there a lot of drug and alcohol abuse in Hollywood today?
ELIJAH: I'm not on drugs. I'm not an alcoholic. I've just got incredible parents and incredible people backing me up. I wouldn't even think about doing drugs. I think it's ridiculous! I think people are throwing their lives away. River Phoenix was such a talented actor. I would have loved to have seen him win an Oscar. He so deserved it. Obviously, he got mixed in with the wrong crowd. That ruined him. I just love life. I've always been this way.

Q: You make a lot of money. Do you spend it on expensive toys, like cars?
ELIJAH: No. Material possessions are only fun for so long and to spend a lot of money on a car just so people will look at you is ridiculous. I'd rather do something to help the homeless or children.

ELIJAH GOT HIS FIRST ACTING JOB JUST SIX WEEKS AFTER MOVING WITH HIS FAMILY FROM CEDAR RAPIDS, IOWA, TO LOS ANGELES.

Q: A lot of people have said there was a rivalry between you and Macaulay Culkin after you made *The Good Son*. Is that true?
ELIJAH: So many people ask that and they think, "Was he a brat, was he this or that?" And I've gotta say no, he was fine. We had a great time.

Q: Do you ever think that you lost some of your childhood by becoming an actor so early in life?
ELIJAH: So many people ask me if I've lost my childhood. Acting for me is normal because it's something that I love to do. And when you're doing

something that you love to do, it's almost like I've created my own childhood, you know what I mean? Because I'm not being forced into it and I'm having a great time.

Q: In *Flipper*, you really enjoyed working with the dolphins. Do you think they really had very different personalities?
ELIJAH: Oh yeah, MacGyver was our hero dolphin, meaning that we used him for all the close-ups and stuff because he was the most beautiful. He would go to the bottom of the ocean and stare at a rock and actually make it look like he was interested in something else. He was a pretty amazing actor....You give them smelt and herring. Every cue you give them, if they do do it correctly, you feed them two or three smelt. That's their positive reinforcement.

Q: In *Deep Impact*, there is a possibility that the world might come to an end. Did you ever think about what you might do if the end was near?
ELIJAH: Oh, yes. The message it gives is that we should all think about our lives and really appreciate what we have. And also, to really live life because you never really know when it could be taken away from you.

Q: Do you think about what you want to be when you are older?
ELIJAH: I like George Lucas because he is a director and a writer. I enjoy writing, and I know that if I can really focus on that and get some good tutoring in English, I can be a really good writer when I get a little older. What's more fun than that? It's creating your own world.

Q: What about seeing you in more romantic roles?
ELIJAH: I'm not ready. And actually it appeals to me more when I see people in their 20s doing [that] stuff rather than kids. Maybe when I'm older.

Q: What's the hardest thing you ever had to do in a movie?
ELIJAH: Kissing. Technically, I had my first on-screen kiss with Jessica Wesson in *Flipper*, but they cut it out. Man, if you want to talk most embarrassing moment...that was it.

It's in the Stars

Elijah Wood
Birthday: January 28, 1981
Star Sign: Aquarius

ELIJAH'S PROFILE:

Elijah's planetary ruler is Uranus, which provides him with waves of spontaneous energy. It's no wonder his family and friends are astounded by his endless enthusiasm and zest for living. Other people get thrown by challenges, but Elijah is someone who actually seeks them out.

The strongest characteristic in Elijah's planetary make-up is his willingness to be unconventional and independent. This actor could have chosen to do projects that would have made him one of the biggest stars on the planet, but Elijah isn't interested in taking the easy way out. He became an actor to challenge himself and his talents, so you'll constantly see him choosing parts that expand his horizons just a little bit and make him a better actor—not a bigger star. His opposite sign is Leo, and like many people, often he is attracted to people who possess qualities quite different from his own. Someone who is calm, peaceful, and introverted might be just the type that catches Elijah's eye, simply because she is not like him and is therefore intriguing.

Elijah shares this talented star sign with other famous people including actress Jennifer Aniston, ballet star Mikhail Baryshnikov, and writer John Grisham. But the fellow Aquarian that would probably impress Elijah the most is Canadian hockey great Wayne Gretzky.

ELIJAH ATTENDED THE LOS ANGELES PREMIERE OF *TITANIC* ON DECEMBER 14, 1997. A LOT OF FANS THINK ELIJAH IS THE TRUE "KING OF THE WORLD."

Girls, Girls, Girls

Elijah melted more than a few hearts when he was seen smooching on the big screen with Christina Ricci in *The Ice Storm*, but says he is still not ready to get carried away with the opposite sex—on the screen or off.

Still, this heartbreaker knows what he likes in a girl. "I look for kindness and intelligence," he says. "I also look for inner and outer beauty." Since his career is in overdrive at the moment, it's hard to find the time to date.

Rest assured, he has been seen out and about with beautiful girls. Elijah admitted to having a bit of a crush on Claire Danes. "She's very talented," he smiles. "I'd love to work with her. I mean, I really loved *My So-Called Life*."

He got to be very close friends with actress Lexi Randall, who played his sister in *The War*. The two shared some interests—they both love movies and the band The Smashing Pumpkins, but the relationship was pretty platonic. "We were put together as brother and sister, and we kind of became like that," Lexi says. "Elijah is always happy. He keeps everything upbeat." Recently, Elijah took Jordana Brewster, who was his costar in *The Faculty*, out with him to the hip New York City club Moomba for a night out on the town. You might remember Jordana as "Nikki" on *As the World Turns*. That night, they went to a big bash hosted by designer Tommy Hilfiger. The duo will also soon be seen wearing Tommy's jeans in a new series of ads. But don't worry because Elijah swears that he and Jordana are just friends!

ABOVE: **ELIJAH WOOD AND THORA BIRCH, COSTARS IN 1991'S *PARADISE*, WERE AN ADORABLE YOUNG DUO. OPPOSITE: ELIJAH SHARES A STEAMY ON-SCREEN KISS WITH CHRISTINA RICCI IN *THE ICE STORM*.**

ELIJAH AND ONE OF THE MOVIE EXTRAS ON THE SET OF *BLACK AND WHITE*.

Being pretty just isn't enough to interest Elijah in a girl. And being a true Midwestern boy at heart, he certainly isn't into any of the extreme and trendy behavior that sometimes passes for fun in Hollywood. "Elijah is a pretty simple guy," says a pal. "He's not into the whole wild Hollywood scene. I think the most important thing he looks for is that the person is nice and decent and thoughtful. Let's face it, you could have the most beautiful face in the world and still be an ugly person. Elijah is the kind of guy who is looking for someone who likes to hang out and have a good time. Someone who doesn't constantly obsess about the way she looks and can relax and have a good laugh.

"He knows that looks might be what initially attracts you to someone, but it isn't enough to keep a romance alive. A great relationship with Elijah would be built on trust, love, and understanding. A girl would have to understand that he has one of the busiest careers in show business right now and that doesn't always give him all the time he would like to have fun. Still, when you were able to see each other, the time would be extra special—because you would have to try to pack so much in the time you have.

"The other thing a girl would simply have to have if she were dating Elijah Wood is a real love of animals," the friend continues. "Elijah loves animals, dogs, cats, horses—and he knows that someone who loves animals truly has a kind heart."

Tons of viewers tuned in to catch a glimpse of Elijah and hear him interviewed when he visited the set of *Live with Regis and Kathie Lee* on December 16, 1998. Elijah blew a kiss to a mystery girl he would only name as "Linda in Los Angeles." "I'm blessed," Elijah explained. "It's unconditional love, the kind of love that you love someone no matter what they do. They take you for everything...for the good and the bad."

For the most part, though, Elijah says he is very careful when it comes to the opposite sex. "It's kind of like a museum where they have those really cool paintings. They're behind the glass and you can look at them, but you can't touch them," he says. "That's what it's like with girls, I can get myself into trouble. And also it's hard because I'm an actor and girls might not like me for who I am. It's hard to deal with."

CHAPTER THREE
THE ROAD TO SUPERSTARDOM

ELIJAH AND THORA BIRCH IN THE 1991 DRAMA *PARADISE*.

Elijah Rising

Elijah Wood is probably the hottest young actor in Hollywood right now, and he certainly has more acting credits than almost anyone else his age. Each movie he has made has led him through a different stage in his development as an actor.

It all started with a role opposite Michael J. Fox in the 1989 sequel *Back to the Future Part II*. It was a small role, but led almost immediately to parts in 1990's *Internal Affairs*, with Jamie Lee Curtis, and *Avalon*, in which he played Aidan Quinn's son in a story about four generations of a Jewish family in Baltimore.

In 1991, Elijah's career really took off with *Paradise*. Still married when they made this movie set in the fictional southern town of Paradise,

Melanie Griffith and Don Johnson play the parents of a sassy and adorable nine-year-old daughter (played by Thora Birch) who are still grieving over the death of another child. Elijah plays Willard, a young boy who is neglected by his own mother and eventually gets shuffled off to live with Griffith and Johnson. But nearly as soon as he arrives, Willard realizes that the place he believed was heaven on earth is really something closer to a war zone for the adults. Griffith's character is so upset about the death of the child that she has a hard time being around her husband. Meanwhile, Johnson's character throws himself so fully into his work (and the local bar) that he has little time left for his family. Eventually, Willard becomes the glue that keeps this delicate family from breaking apart.

"This kid is absolutely wonderful," actor Michael Douglas said when he saw Elijah's performance.

Paradise was quickly followed by 1992's *Radio Flyer*. While making that movie, Elijah told an interviewer, "This is probably one of the best movies

IN THE 1991 FILM *PARADISE*, ELIJAH PLAYS WILLARD YOUNG, THE LOVABLE KID WHO SHOWS LILY AND BEN REED (MELANIE GRIFFITH AND DON JOHNSON) HOW TO LIVE AGAIN AFTER SUFFERING A TRAGIC LOSS.

I've done, because it's a good role, and I get to work with dogs." The film is a fantasy set in the 1960s about two brothers (Elijah and Joseph Mazzello) who are being physically abused by their stepfather. Their mom, played by actress Lorraine Bracco, is completely oblivious to what's going on. The boys cope by drifting off into a fantasy world that includes their German shepherd, Shane, a pet turtle, and a Radio Flyer wagon that they imagine is a flying machine. Elijah plays Mike, a little boy who has to fight to be strong and to survive all the terrible things he is going through.

IN 1992'S *RADIO FLYER*, ELIJAH TOOK ON ONE OF HIS EARLIEST EMOTIONALLY CHALLENGING ACTING PARTS.

"Elijah was so pure," says director Richard Donner. "He was so pure, so naive. You look through his eyes, and you see no harm, no pain—nothing but happiness."

In 1992, Elijah really hit it off playing opposite Mel Gibson in *Forever Young*. Even though the movie was a serious drama, Elijah says he really enjoyed hanging out with Mel off camera. "Mel is so much fun to be around," Elijah says. "He goofed around like a kid and just made it more comfortable for everyone around him. I learned a lot from him." The movie tells the story of a test pilot (played by Gibson) whose girlfriend is left in a coma after a car accident.

BELOW: ELIJAH, LORRAINE BRACCO, AND JOSEPH MAZZELLO—A WIDOWED MOTHER AND HER SONS IN *RADIO FLYER*. PAGES 38–39: ELIJAH AND HIS FILM BROTHER JOSEPH MAZZELLO HAVE FUN WITH A TURTLE ON THE SET OF *RADIO FLYER*.

BELOW: ELIJAH LEARNED EVERYTHING HE NEEDED TO KNOW ABOUT PRACTICAL JOKING FROM MEL GIBSON, HIS COSTAR IN THE 1992 FILM *FOREVER YOUNG*. RIGHT: IN *FOREVER YOUNG*, NAT (ELIJAH WOOD) TEACHES DANIEL (MEL GIBSON) ABOUT SOME OF THE INVENTIONS THAT THE LATTER HAS MISSED DURING THE PAST FIFTY YEARS.

He volunteers to be frozen as part of a cryogenics experiment. But he is accidentally thawed out in 1992, and among the first people he encounters are a young boy (played by Elijah) and his mom (played by Jamie Lee Curtis). In this romantic fantasy, Mel ends up winning the hearts of the girl and the kid.

Elijah and his parents decided that the best move for him in 1993 would be to bring one of the classics to the big screen. So he took the lead in the film version of a Mark Twain classic, *The Adventures of Huck Finn*, which he filmed when he was just twelve years old. To prepare for the role, Elijah read Twain's *The Adventures of Tom Sawyer* and *The Adventures of Huckleberry Finn*. What he wasn't ready for, though, was the scene where he had to smoke a pipe. "It had some kind of herb in it," Elijah recalls. "They didn't let me inhale. I just put it in my mouth and kind of blew out the smoke. It was fun, but kind of gross."

Elijah said he loved playing the part of a timeless American boy. "I don't think I'm like him," Elijah said at the time. "I don't lie to get out of trouble. I don't do that kind of stuff. He didn't really have a father. His father was, like, an alcoholic and beat him a lot. And his mother died too, so he was kind of on his own. Huck had a lot of heart; he tried to do the right thing. He was a real good thinker, too, because when he had conclusions, he thought them out himself."

From an American classic, Elijah moved on to a role that surprised and upset some people. At the time the movie was made, Macaulay Culkin was the hottest child actor in America. The film came hot on the heels of his *Home Alone* success, and everyone was waiting to see what Mac would do next.

The result was 1993's *The Good Son*, in which Macaulay Culkin plays a bad kid; Elijah is his good little cousin and the only one who sees the evil under the surface.

OPPOSITE: ELIJAH WAS ALREADY A SEASONED ACTOR IN 1993 WHEN HE STARRED IN *THE ADVENTURES OF HUCK FINN*. HIS PERFORMANCE WON HIM RAVE REVIEWS. ABOVE: ELIJAH WAS JUST TWELVE YEARS OLD WHEN HE COSTARRED WITH ACTOR COURTNEY B. VANCE, WHO PLAYED JIM IN *THE ADVENTURES OF HUCK FINN*.

Elijah on the Small Screen

On the small screen, there have been numerous television appearances for Elijah. When he was just thirteen, he made his first appearance on *Late Night with David Letterman*, and he completely wowed the host with his amazing maturity and quick wit. He dissolved into complete silliness on *The Tonight Show with Jay Leno* when he and Jay Frasier Crane. He was seen by almost 80 million people when he was part of the half-time show during SuperBowl XXVIII in a commercial with former Vice President Dan Quayle and Dallas Cowboy star quarterback Troy Aikman.

If you are a true Elijah Wood fan, you might want to check out the book on tape,

ended up spraying each other with cans of silly string. Elijah's acting was hailed by critics when he guest-starred in a 1993 episode of *Homicide: Life on the Street*. Elijah, in the role of McPhee Broadman, a cocky prep school student suspected of murder, gives a chilling performance in this award-winning television drama. On *Frasier*, Elijah got laughs as one of the radio call-ins to Dr. *The Most Beautiful Gift* (Time Warner Audio-Books). Elijah is the narrator of this lovely Christmas fable by author Jonathan Snow. It tells the story of a lonely boy who captures the world's most beautiful snowflake and decides he's going to give it to the kindest person in the world. Through his journey, he finally learns what the true spirit of the holidays is all about.

OPPOSITE: ELIJAH WAS NICKNAMED "MONKEY" WHEN HE WAS A KID, AND HE BONDED WITH THIS CUTE LITTLE GUY AT THE *9TH ANNUAL KIDS' CHOICE AWARDS*. ABOVE: ELIJAH AT THE 1996 PREMIERE OF *FLIPPER*. PAGES 46–47: THEY PLAYED ENEMIES ON CAMERA IN *THE GOOD SON*, BUT IN REAL LIFE ELIJAH AND MACAULAY CULKIN HUNG OUT TOGETHER.

MACAULAY AND ELIJAH BECAME GOOD PALS ON THE SET. AT THE TIME, MACAULAY WAS ONE OF THE HOTTEST YOUNG STARS IN THE WORLD.

ABOVE: *THE GOOD SON* WAS THE FIRST SCARY MOVIE THAT ELIJAH ACTED IN. PAGES 50–51: ELIJAH SAYS HE GOT ALONG REALLY WELL WITH KEVIN COSTNER, WHO PLAYED HIS DAD IN 1994'S *THE WAR*. "HE'S A GREAT GUY," ELIJAH SAYS.

"It was really scary to make," Elijah says. "Mac plays the bad seed. He's a psychologically messed-up kid. He pretends to be sweet, but he's got this infatuation with death. He loves killing things. I try to tell everybody, but they don't believe me. They think I'm the disturbed one. It's weird. You think you can trust kids. Not always...not all of them."

The two actors became friends on the set and spent time at each other's houses. "Mac is a nice kid," Elijah says. "He knows a lot. He's lots of fun to work with and be around."

Next up for Elijah came *The War* in 1994. Kevin Costner plays Southerner Stephen Simmons, a Vietnam veteran who is having a hard time leaving the war behind and learning to be with his wife and children again. Elijah plays his young son Stu, a charming boy who is working hard to keep the family together. When he's not dealing with his father, Stu has to try to stop town bullies from harassing him and his sister Lidia (Lexi Randall). The film's big scene comes when Stu and Lidia have to fight the bullies over their own tree house. Elijah says that he hopes people got the message of the movie, which he sums up thoughtfully, "In the absence of love, there's nothing worth fighting for.

That message is very important to me, because there is so much violence in our world these days. The message of the movie makes sense, and I think it's very, very important for kids to see. Adults will understand the message, but I think it's too late to change anything, they're already too set in their ways. But kids still have a chance to change things, and that's why I want them to see it."

A lot of people predicted that Elijah's first starring role in 1994, *North*, would be a big hit because of Elijah and director Rob Reiner. The movie was a comedy about an eleven-year-old boy named North (played by Elijah) who wants to divorce his parents. In the movie, Jason Alexander and Julia Louis-Dreyfus (both from TV's *Seinfeld*) play North's parents, who just don't pay enough attention to him. So North travels the globe from Texas to China to Alaska to Hawaii to find new parents. (In Paris, he discovers he could never live there because all the people around him watch Jerry Lewis movies.)

Although the movie bombed, nearly all the critics who reviewed it said the best thing about it was...Elijah Wood. He also managed to really impress

IN *THE WAR*, LEXI RANDALL, ELIJAH, AND LATOYA CHISHOLM PLAY BEST BUDS, WHO ARE DETERMINED TO STOP THE TOWN'S BULLIES FROM HARASSING THEM.

ELIJAH IN *THE WAR*. WHAT HAPPENED TO THOSE CURLY, BROWN LOCKS OF HAIR?

LEXI RANDALL, ELIJAH, AND MARE WINNINGHAM, ON THE SET OF THE WAR.

one of his costars. "He's like a little man inside of a boy's body," says actress Faith Ford. "One minute he can be playing and the next minute he's just as believable as anything."

The failure of that film is just another thing that Elijah takes in stride. "It doesn't affect me. I do a film. I do my best," he says. "I try to promote it the best I can, I see the film, and that's it. I don't wait to see if it becomes number one. If it bombs, it's no tragedy. I'm done with the film, so I don't think about it."

NORTH'S PARENTS (PLAYED BY JASON ALEXANDER AND JULIA LOUIS-DREYFUS) HAVE A HEART-TO-HEART TALK WITH THEIR PRECOCIOUS ELEVEN-YEAR-OLD SON.

Elijah rebounded in 1996 with *Flipper*, which was a hit. People around the world were touched by this remake of the enduring NBC TV series. Elijah plays Sandy Ricks, a rebellious young boy sent to spend the summer with his Uncle Porter (played by Paul Hogan). Porter is an *ex-hippie* who worked as a roadie for The Beach Boys before dropping out to become a fisherman. At first, Sandy finds the whole trip unbearably boring—until he meets up with an orphan dolphin named "Flipper," who becomes his best friend. "Elijah Wood was the perfect Sandy," says the movie's producer Perry Katz. "We needed a seasoned young actor who could portray a complicated character.

NORTH HITS THE ROAD TO FIND PARENTS WHO WILL REALLY LOVE HIM.

ELIJAH AND BRUCE WILLIS GET BUNDLED UP FOR THEIR TRAVELS THROUGH ALASKA IN *NORTH*.

IN 1994, ELIJAH WENT TO LAS VEGAS TO ACCEPT HIS AWARD AS SHOWEST'S YOUNG STAR OF THE YEAR.

Sandy has tremendous movement in his character. He goes from spoiled urban city kid with a chip on his shoulder to a kid who, through his contact with a dolphin, learns about life and begins to bridge into adulthood."

The movie was shot in the Bahamas, and in order to swim with the dolphins, Elijah was trained in skin diving, holding his breath, and various swimming techniques. "Working with these dolphins was one of the most rewarding things I ever did," Elijah says. "To gain their confidence, I began feeding them and learning how to communicate with them and swimming with them. They know that you trust them and they learn to trust you. It's incredible to walk on the dock and have Jake, for example, run up to me, whip his tail, and let me know he is glad to see me. It's amazing to be recognized and loved by them. I missed them after the movie was finished, because they became my friends."

ELIJAH LOOKED EVERY BIT THE HOLLYWOOD STAR AT THE 1994 ACADEMY AWARDS CEREMONY.

The one thing he didn't love was the character of Sandy. "I think that Sandy is a negative person. A real brat," he said while making the movie. "But because he changes in the movie, I thought it would be a real challenge to play the role."

Elijah's next film, in 1997, was a definite departure from anything else he had ever done. In *The Ice Storm*, Elijah really challenged himself with a tough dramatic part. Alongside Kevin Kline, Joan Allen, Sigourney Weaver, and pal Christina Ricci, Elijah starred as Mikey in a movie about a family struggling to survive in the turbulent 1970s.

Kevin Kline is a seemingly happy dad married to Joan Allen. The audience soon learns, though, that he is in the midst of a steamy affair with his bored

"Acting for me is normal because it's something I love to do."

OPPOSITE: **ELIJAH GIVES THE CAMERAS A BIG THUMBS-UP AT THE 1994 ACADEMY AWARDS CEREMONY.**

BY 1996, WHEN HE WAS PROMOTING *FLIPPER*, ELIJAH WAS ALREADY A VETERAN OF ELEVEN MOVIES.

ELIJAH SAYS THE DOLPHINS REALLY GOT TO KNOW HIM, AND HE GOT TO UNDERSTAND ALL OF THEIR DIFFERENT PERSONALITIES ON THE SET OF *FLIPPER* IN 1996. "YOU BUILD A BOND OF TRUST WITH THE DOLPHINS," ELIJAH SAYS.

neighbor, Janey (Sigourney Weaver). Elijah plays one of Janey's two young sons (Adam Hann-Byrd plays the other). In this complicated story, both boys explore their emerging sexuality with Kline's daughter, who is played by Christina Ricci.

When Kline's wife learns of his affair, she is hurt and angry. At a neighborhood party during a severe ice storm, she suspects that her husband and neighbor are going to try to get together during a partner swapping interlude. Not long after, a tragedy occurs because of the ice storm. Ultimately, all the adults involved are forced to examine their own selfish behavior.

"The whole idea of sex was just completely different then," Elijah says. "It was different from the '60s in that it wasn't necessarily about free love, but it was still about experimentation. I was completely shocked by the whole partner-swapping thing. It blew me away, and I couldn't believe that it not only existed but that couples were cool with it. That really surprised me."

Thinking about the moral decisions that his character has to make was definitely a challenge in this very adult role. "I actually had to sit and think about my character and really develop him," says Elijah. "That started my move to being an adult actor."

A BOY AND HIS DOLPHIN—ELIJAH FEEDS FLIPPER.

ELIJAH SWIMS WITH HIS DOLPHIN COSTAR IN *FLIPPER*.

In 1998, Elijah starred in *Deep Impact* with Robert Duvall, Téa Leoni, Morgan Freeman—and a very, very big comet headed straight for Earth! Elijah plays fourteen-year-old Leo Biederman, who joins the high school astronomy club with the hope of getting the attention of his classmate Sarah Hotchner (played by Leelee Sobieski). Instead he takes a photograph through his telescope and discovers a comet, although he first thinks it is just a simple shooting star. But, boy, is he wrong! Ultimately, a world-weary astronaut (played by Duvall) is called upon to help save the world.

Yet again in 1998, Elijah won a tough part, this time in a movie called *The Bumblebee Flies Away* (released in 1999). "It's basically a movie about a last-ditch treatment center for terminally ill children," Elijah says. He plays Barney Snow, a boy with amnesia trapped in a depressing cancer research center. While he's there, he is surrounded by such characters as tough-talking street kid Billy the Kidney (George Gore) and a boy called Mazzo (Joe Perrino), who is stuck in a hospital bed after two intentional car wrecks.

The year 1998 was a busy one for Elijah, who got his first shot at acting in one of those horror movies that he loves so much. In *The Faculty*, he plays Casey, one of a group of hip teens who are trying to save the world from some very scary teachers whose bodies have been invaded by aliens.

The movie was written by *Dawson's Creek* creator Kevin Williamson and costars Jordana Brewster, *Halloween: H20*'s Josh Hartnett, and singer Usher.

Director Robert Rodriguez gushed about working with Elijah Wood. "Elijah Wood is the coolest kid I've ever met," he says. "He has been in the business longer than most people, and he's still enthusiastic and confident. He's very charming, generous, and genuine."

Elijah said making this movie with a group of young friends was more like a party than a movie set. "Yeah, it was basically like going away to summer camp," he said. "Except you're doing scenes where you have to freak out and run from scary objects, and there's blood and stuff."

While working on *The Faculty* was a great deal of fun for Elijah, there was also a lot of hard work involved. Elijah plays a character who is completely insecure. "I'm just not insecure in real life," he says. But then again, that's what acting is all about.

ELIJAH IN 1997'S *THE ICE STORM*.

ELIJAH SAYS THAT *THE ICE STORM* WAS ONE OF HIS MOST DEMANDING ROLES TO DATE.

There was a lot of good-natured teasing on the set of this flick. One night the entire cast went out to dinner, and the waiter recognized Elijah and called him "Mr. Wood." Elijah's new costars Jordana Brewster, Josh Hartnett, and Shawn Hatosy got a big kick out of this. "They were continually calling me `Mr. Wood,' just to be on my case about it," he says.

With each new film or project, Elijah likes to try something a little different to expand his talents. And 1999's *Black and White* is no exception. This strange tale is a real departure from the kinds of films that Elijah has done so far. Robert Downey, Jr., plays Brooke Shields's gay husband, who is also a documentary filmmaker. Downey's character decides to film a group of Manhattan kids who just love hip-hop music. Elijah is one of the hip-hop wannabes, along with Bijoux Phillips. Ben Stiller is on hand playing a New York City detective, and even boxer Mike Tyson makes an appearance playing...who else? Mike Tyson.

"I've been progressively going into more adult roles, trying more and more challenging roles."

OPPOSITE AND ABOVE: **ELIJAH SPORTS THE PREPPY LOOK.** PAGES 70–71: **ELIJAH TEARS THROUGH THE STREETS DURING A TENSE MOMENT IN** *DEEP IMPACT*.

ELIJAH HELPS TO SAVE THE WORLD IN 1998'S DISASTER MOVIE *DEEP IMPACT*.

ABOVE: ELIJAH HOLDS ON TO LEELEE SOBIESKI (WHO PLAYS SARAH) AS THE END SEEMS NEAR IN *DEEP IMPACT*. PAGES 74–75: LEELEE SOBIESKI AND ELIJAH HIT THE ROAD AND TRY TO OUTRUN THE COMET THAT'S COMING TO SQUASH THEM IN *DEEP IMPACT*.

ELIJAH PLAYED OPPOSITE RICHARD DREYFUSS IN THE 1997 TELEVISION VERSION OF THE CHARLES DICKENS CLASSIC *OLIVER TWIST*.

ELIJAH WAS HONORED FOR HIS PORTRAYAL OF THE ARTFUL DODGER IN *OLIVER TWIST* AT THE 3RD ANNUAL *HOLLYWOOD REPORTER* YOUNG STAR AWARDS.

"I never wanted to act to become famous. I just enjoy acting."

OPPOSITE AND ABOVE: ELIJAH WORE A PAIR OF RETRO SHADES TO THE HOLLYWOOD PREMIERE OF THE SEVENTIES-THEMED FLICK *54*. PAGES 80–81: ELIJAH AND USHER LOOKING SUSPICIOUS IN THE 1998 HORROR FILM *THE FACULTY*.

Elijah Wood

IN *THE FACULTY*, ELIJAH AND COSTAR JORDANA BREWSTER TEAM UP TO UNRAVEL THE MYSTERY THAT HAS THROWN HERRINGTON HIGH SCHOOL INTO A PANIC.

ABOVE: **SHAWN HATOSY, LAURA HARRIS, JOSH HARTNETT, JORDANA BREWSTER, CLEA DUVALL, AND ELIJAH IN** *THE FACULTY*.
PAGES 84–85: **THE STUDENTS OF HERRINGTON HIGH HAVE GOOD REASON TO WORRY—AND NOT JUST ABOUT THEIR HOMEWORK!**

CHAPTER FOUR
THE ROAD AHEAD

Like most teenagers, Elijah Wood can't wait to grow up. He says he has had the best childhood that anyone could possibly imagine, but he's ready to become an adult and take on the world.

At the moment, he is concerned with college and whether or not he'll go to film school. "I'm very pleased at the way my career has been going," he says. "I've been progressively going into more adult roles, trying more and more challenging roles. For me, that's very important."

One of Elijah's plans for the near future involves a big change in location. He hopes to move all the way across the country. Elijah says he wants to move to Manhattan and hopes to be accepted at Columbia University, where he'd study English.

"I live in Los Angeles, but I love New York. I'm going to move there in a year," he says. "I live with Mom and Dad right now. My mom's always been there for me. I've had a lot of love in my life."

Still, growing up is tough. It's hard on his parents, too, especially his mom, who is used to traveling everywhere with Elijah and being totally involved in his life. He says his parents are slowly handing over the reins to him so he can make his own decisions.

"Most nights I get home late, but it's cool with them," he says. "The independence thing is sort of happening. It's gradual and good. It's a difficult process for my parents, but it's happening."

But don't think Elijah is going to give up his career while he's in New York studying. He wants to go to school and take time off when really good acting parts come his way. "I'm going to fifty-fifty it," he laughs.

School, with hundreds of other students around him day after day, will be a major adjustment for Elijah, who has spent most of his education being home-schooled. He says he doesn't think he really missed out on anything by being home-schooled, and if anything, he got to skip a lot of the cattiness of being in the "right" crowd. "The school crowd bothers me," he says. "I'd probably find someone that didn't like any of that and hang out with them if I went to a public school. Then again, that would be our clique, so there's no way out of it."

ELIJAH WENT TO SEE THE MOVIE *SCREAM 2* AS SOON AS IT OPENED IN 1997. HE'S A SELF-CONFESSED HORROR MOVIE JUNKIE.

"I want to show people my passion through thought-provoking films."

OPPOSITE AND ABOVE: **ELIJAH AT THE HOLLYWOOD PREMIERE OF** *TITANIC* **IN 1997.**

Ultimately, Elijah says he would like to write and direct a movie and thinks he is certainly on the right track to accomplish his dream. "I want to show people my passion through thought-provoking films," he says.

It looks like Elijah is certainly living up to the praise he received from film critic Roger Ebert, who heralded Elijah, "the most talented actor in his age group in Hollywood history."

ABOVE: ELIJAH AND MOVIE EXTRAS TAKE A BREAK FROM SHOOTING *BLACK AND WHITE* TO POSE FOR THE CAMERA. OPPOSITE: ELIJAH ON LOCATION IN NEW YORK CITY FOR THE HIP AND CONTROVERSIAL MOVIE *BLACK AND WHITE*.

Filmography

VIDEO PROJECTS: "Forever Your Girl" with Paula Abdul
"Ridiculous Thoughts" with The Cranberries

TV: *Homicide: Life on the Street* (NBC)

Day-O (NBC)

Oliver Twist (ABC)

Child in the Night (CBS)

The Witness (Showtime)

Frasier (NBC)

Storytime (PBS)

Adventures from the Book of Virtues (PBS)

The Hollywood Christmas Parade (KTLA)

The Family Film Awards (CBS)

9th Annual Kids' Choice Awards (Nickelodeon)

Young Musicians Symphony Orchestra Special (Disney Channel)

The 66th Annual Academy Awards (ABC)

MOVIES: *Back to the Future Part II* (1989)

Internal Affairs (1990)

Avalon (1990)

Paradise (1991)

Radio Flyer (1992)

Forever Young (1992)

The Good Son (1993)

The Adventures of Huck Finn (1993)

The War (1994)

North (1994)

Flipper (1996)

The Ice Storm (1997)

Deep Impact (1998)

The Faculty (1998)

Black and White (1999)

The Bumblebee Flies Anyway (1999)

Bibliography

Ansen, David. "The Wife Swappers." *Time*. (September 29, 1997): 72.

Bernard, Jamie. "North Follows the Bouncing Offspring, Goes Boing." *New York Daily News*. (July 22, 1994): 20.

Browne, N.P. "Elijah Wood: 'I'm Going to Be a Kid as Long as I Can.'" *Women's World*. (January 24, 1995): 12.

Burr, Ty. "The Revelations of Elijah." *Entertainment Weekly*. (November 25, 1994): 38-39.

Clarke, John. "Location Scout." *New York Post*. (February 15, 1998): 64.

Connors, Claire. "On Elijah Wood." *Sassy*. (June, 1996): 33.

Elliott, Stuart. "Frito-Lay Puts Its Cowboy on 2 Horses at Same Time." *New York Times*. (December 29, 1994): D19.

Fierman, Daniel. "The Fright Stuff." *Entertainment Weekly*. (November 20, 1998): 54-60.

"Five More Rising Stars." *USA Today*. (October 16, 1991): D2.

"From Soaps to The Silver Screen." *Soap Opera Update*. (June 23, 1998): 12.

Gardella, Kay. "In Doing the Twist, Disney's Only Fagin It." *New York Daily News*. (November 15, 1997): 63.

Green, Tom. "A Down-to-Earth Huck." *USA Today*. (April 5, 1993): 1D-2D.

Griffin, Nancy. "Actor Elijah Wood." *Premiere*. (March 1992): 47.

Guillo, Jim. "Splashback." *Premiere*. (May 1996): 25-26.

"The Hot Kids of Summer." *New York Times*. (June 17, 1993): 10.

Howe, Desson. "Family Trouble in Paradise." *Washington Post*. (October 4, 1991): D4.

Johnson, Allan. "Ahh, Leave Him Alone." *Chicago Tribune*. (November 8, 1994): 45.

Johnson, Steve. "Channel Surfing." *Chicago Tribune*. (November 22, 1996): 6.

Maslin, Janet. "Family Values and Love in Vietnam Aftermath." *New York Times*. (November 4, 1994): D8.

——————. "Huck Finn and Jim Drifting Together." *New York Times*. (April 2, 1993): D6.

Mills, Bart. "A New Boy Wonder." *New York Daily News*. (April 4, 1993): 19.

Mills, Bart. "The Boy Who Would Be Finn." *TV Host*. (June 1994): 6A.

Moy, Suelain. "Well Trained at Twelve." *Entertainment Weekly*. (April 2, 1993): 61.

"No Display Case." *People Magazine*. (May 27, 1996): 10.

Oldenburg, Ann. "Teen Star Growing into His Own Man." *USA Today*. (November 4, 1994): 2D.

"Openings." *USA Today*. (September 17, 1991): D3.

O'Toole, Leslie. "Live Life—Because You Never Know When It Could Be Taken Away." *Neon*. (June 1998): 18.

Pearlman, Cindy. "The Big Picture." *Chicago Sun-Times*. (July 4, 1997): 12.

Puig, Claudia. "Elijah Wood." *USA Today*. (October 22, 1997): F6.

Rauzi, Robin. "Elijah Wood: Having Fun as a Kid." *Los Angeles Times*. (April 6, 1993): F1-F3.

———. "A Star But Still a Kid." *Los Angeles Times*. (April 20, 1993): 70.

Schaefer, Stephen. "Melancholy Macaulay Has Quit Flicks: Pal." *New York Daily News*. (April 30, 1996): 10.

"Short Takes." *Soap Opera Magazine*. (April 7, 1998): 12.

Vander Pluym, Andre. "Elijah Wood." *Teen Magazine*. (February 1998): 17.

Winters, Patricia. "Spud Stud Quayle in Super Bowl Chip Shot." *New York Daily News*. (January 28, 1994): 16.

Wolf, Jean. "In the Swim." *TV Guide*. (June 1, 1996): 44.

Photo Credits

Archive Photos: ©Lee: p. 58

Camera Press/Retna Limited U.S.A.: p. 57; ©Theodore Wood: p. 8

Corbis: ©Omega: back jacket, p. 26; ©Pacha: front jacket, pp. 5 left, 25, 68, 69, 88; ©Frank Ross: pp. 32, 90, 91

Deider Davidson/Saga/Archive Photos: p. 29

The Everett Collection: pp. 5 right, 15, 16-17, 18, 19, 34, 35, 40, 41, 42, 65, 66, 67, 70-71, 72, 76

Globe Photos Inc.: ©Tom Rodriguez: p. 23; ©Lisa Rose: pp. 2, 87

London Features International, U.S.A: ©Gregg DeGuire: pp. 24, 27, 45, 59, 78; ©Nick Elgar: pp. 21, 30; ©Allen Gordon: p. 13

Photofest: pp. 6-7, 14, 31, 36, 37, 38-39, 43, 46-47, 48, 49, 50-51, 52, 53, 54, 55, 56, 63, 64, 73, 74-75, 77, 80-81, 82, 83, 84-85

Retna Limited U.S.A.: ©Steve Granitz: pp. 60, 61; ©Greg Pace: p. 62; ©Barry Talesnick: p. 9

Jim Smeal/Galella Ltd.: pp. 11, 20, 22, 44, 89

Index

A
Abdul, Paula, 14–15
Address for correspondence, 9
The Adventures of Huck Finn, 42, 43, *43*
Animals, 8, 9, 33
Auditions, 10–14
Avalon, 14, 15, *15*, 16–17, 34
Awards, 9, 44, 58, 59, 60–61

B
Back to the Future Part II, 15, 34
Birch, Thora, *30*, 34, 35
Black and White, 32, 67, 92, 93
Books, 9, 13, 43
Bracco, Lorraine, 37
Brewster, Jordana, 30, *82*, 83
Brother, 9, 20
The Bumblebee Flies Away, 65
Burke, Delta, *18*, 19

C
Charisma, 10
Chisholm, Latoya, *52*
Correspondence
  address for, 9
Costner, Kevin, 49, 50–51
Culkin, Macaulay, 22, 27, 43, 46–47, 48

D
Danes, Claire, 30
Day-O, 18, 19
Deep Impact, 28, 65, 70–71, 72, 73, 74–75

Donner, Richard, 36
Douglas, Michael, 35
Dreyfuss, Richard, 76
Drugs, 27

E
Ebert, Roger, 92

F
Fact File, 9
The Faculty, 6, 65–67, 80–81, 82, 83, 84–85
Fame, 25
Family, 9, 20–23, 25
Flipper, 13, 28, 55–59, 63, 64, 65
Ford, Faith, 55
Forever Young, 36–43, *40*, *41*
"Forever Your Girl," video for, 14–15
Frasier, 44
Friends, 25–27, 66
Fun Facts, 12–13
Future plans, 86

G
Gibson, Mel, 36, *40*, *41*
Girls, 30–33
The Good Son, 22, 43–44, 46–47, 49
Griffith, Melanie, 35, *35*

H
Hannah, 9, 20, *20*, 22, *22–23*, *23*
Hobbies, 9
Hollywood, 10
Homicide: Life on the Street, 44

I

The Ice Storm, 30, 59–64, 66, 67

Internal Affairs, 15, 34

Interviews, 24–25, 33

J

Johnson, Don, 35, *35*

K

Katz, Perry, 55

Kissing, 28, *31*

L

Late Night with David Letterman, 44

Lucas, George, 13

M

Mazzello, Joseph, 36, *36*, *37*, *38–39*

Money, 12, 27

The Most Beautiful Gift, 44

Mother, 10, 14, 20–22, *21*, 25, 86

Music, 9, 12

N

Nicknames, 9, 12

North, 12, 52–55, *55*, *56*, *57*

  promotion of, *8*

O

Oliver Twist, 76, 77

P

Paradise, 30, 34, 34–35, *35*

Parents, 9

Pets, 8, 9

Preppy look, 68–69

Promotions, *8*, *9*, 62

Q

Quinn, Aidan, 15, *16–17*

R

Radio Flyer, 35–36, *36*, *37*, *38–39*

Randall, Lexi, 30, 49, *52*, 54

Retro look, 78–79

Ricci, Christina, 30, *31*, 64

Rodriguez, Robert, 66

Romantic roles, 28, 30, *31*

S

Scalzo, Gary, 10, 15

Sister, 9, 20, *20*, 22, *22–23*, *23*

Stahl, Armin Mueller, *14*

Star sign, 29

Swardstrom, Brian, 20

T

Talent, 10

Television appearances, 44

W

The War, 12, 49–52, *50–51*, *52*, *53*, 54

Wesson, Jessica, 28

Willis, Bruce, 57

Z

Zach, 9, 20